Anybody for

by C.B. Gilford

Baker's Plays
7611 Sunset Blvd.
Los Angeles, CA 90042
bakersplays.com

NOTICE

This book is offered for sale at the price quoted only on the understanding that, if any additional copies of the whole or any part are necessary for its production, such additional copies will be purchased. The attention of all purchasers is directed to the following: this work is fully protected under the copyright laws of the United States of America, the British Commonwealth, including Canada, and all other countries of the Copyright Union. Violations of the Copyright Law are punishable by fine or imprisonment, or both. The copying or duplication of this work or any part of this work, by hand or by any process, is an infringement of the copyright and will be vigorously prosecuted.

This play may not be produced by amateurs or professionals for public or private performance without first submitting application for performing rights. Licensing fees are due on all performances whether for charity or gain, or whether admission is charged or not. Since performance of this play without the payment of the licensing fee renders anybody participating liable to severe penalties imposed by the law, anybody acting in this play should be sure, before doing so, that the licensing fee has been paid. Professional rights, reading rights, radio broadcasting, television and all mechanical rights, etc. are strictly reserved. Application for performing rights should be made directly to BAKER'S PLAYS.

No one shall commit or authorize any act or omission by which the copyright of, or the right to copyright, this play may be impaired. No one shall make any changes in this play for the purpose of production.

Publication of this play does not imply availability for performance. Both amateurs and professionals considering a production are strongly advised in their own interest to apply to Baker's Plays for written permission before starting rehearsals, advertising, or booking a theatre.

Whenever the play is produced, the author's name must be carried in all publicity, advertising and programs. Also, the following notice must appear on all printed programs, "Produced by special arrangement with Baker's Plays."

Licensing fees for ANYBODY FOR TEA? are based on a per performance rate and payable one week in advance of the production.

Please consult the Baker's Plays website at www.bakersplays.com or our current print catalogue for up to date licensing fee information.

ANYBODY FOR TEA?
ISBN **978-0-87440-951-2**
#113-B

STORY OF THE PLAY

Detective Dennis O'Finn, investigating the death of an elderly lady, discovers that he is the motive for the murder. Six sweet but balmy spinsters are all in love with their bachelor neighbor, the handsome fortyish O'Finn. To get him to visit them, they stage a homicide. To keep him around, another one must be arranged. Based on the successful three-acter, BULL IN A CHINA SHOP, this charming chiller is a top contest play.

CAST

CAPTAIN WILLIAMS

DENNIS O'FINN

MISS HILDEGARDE

MISS BIRDIE

MISS AMANTHA

MISS LUCY

MISS NETTIE

MISS ELIZABETH

KRAMER

Any Body for Tea?

SCENE: Action on the forestage is in the office of Captain
Williams of the Metropolitan Police Force. The
full stage is the Victorian house of Hildegarde
Hodge, a boarding house for elderly spinsters.

*The house and the stage are black. Then suddenly a light
shows, a small light, in a goose-neck lamp sitting on a
very small desk at Downstage Right, on the apron of the
stage. By its illumination we see that the act curtain is
down. Behind the desk sits a portly man in a plain business suit, CAPTAIN WILLIAMS of the Metropolitan
Police Force. Standing before the desk is DENNIS
O'FINN, a well-built man of forty, wearing an Irish
smile, and plain, not too well-pressed clothes. His hat is
in his hand. The light of the lamp shines downward, fo-
cused on a stack of papers on the desk, and not reveal-
ing too much of either of the men's faces.*

WILLIAMS. (*Irritably*) O'Finn, what do you want?
Don't you realize it's midnight?
O'FINN. I know it is, Captain Williams, but I saw the
light on in your office here and I thought it'd be all right.
. . .
WILLIAMS. Well, what is it? I'm a busy man.
O'FINN. It's my request for transfer, sir.
WILLIAMS. Oh yes, that silly business. (*Digs out paper
from the stack and reads excerpts from it aloud*) Dennis
Patrick O'Finn . . . age forty . . . bachelor . . . twelve
years in uniform on the beat . . . seven years Homicide
Division . . . present rank, Detective First Class . . . re-
quests transfer to Arson Squad . . . (*Looks up*) O'Finn,
do you even know what the Arson Squad does?
O'FINN. It investigates fires, sir.
WILLIAMS. Good. (*Reading again*) Reasons for request

5

. . . personal. (*Looks up again*) Would you explain that, O'Finn?

O'FINN. It's private personal, captain.

WILLIAMS. (*Leans back and studies* O'FINN) O'Finn, you've seven years experience in Homicide. You're no Sherlock Holmes, but you seem to have the luck of the Irish, so you've done a good job. We don't need anybody in Arson, so why should I transfer you?

O'FINN. Please, Captain. It's a matter of life and death.

WILLIAMS. Explain.

O'FINN. Do I have to?

WILLIAMS. If you want the transfer.

O'FINN. (*Takes a moment to decide*) Captain, will you keep this confidential?

WILLIAMS. Of course I will.

O'FINN. Word of honor?

WILLIAMS. Word of honor.

O'FINN. Well then, Captain, it was like this. There was this house, you see. 909 Sycamore. A house about a hundred years old. But it's right straight across the street from the apartment building where I live. And it being nice weather, I left the window and the shade up when I was shaving. Now in this house there were six old spinster ladies . . .

(*During the above speech, the curtain has risen slowly and silently, and now, at* O'FINN's *last sentence, the stage lights come up. We see the tableau of the six ladies,* MISS HILDEGARDE, *the landlady,* MISS BIRDIE, MISS AMANTHA, MISS LUCY, MISS NETTIE *and* MISS ELIZABETH. *They are inhabiting an old-fashioned parlor which features a sofa, several chairs, a tea table, and some spinsterish knickknacks, such as a canary in a cage. Downstage left is a window, or a suggestion of a window. Up left is the doorway to the front hall. Up right is the doorway to the kitchen. The tableau consists of* ELIZABETH, *standing on a chair, looking out the window through a pair of binoculars, and the others clustered around her.*)

O'FINN. Peeping Toms, that's what they were, Captain.

(O'FINN *freezes and stays that way through the ensuing scene. The ladies spring into action.*)

AMANTHA. Elizabeth, what's he doing now?

ELIZABETH. He's in his undershirt.

BIRDIE. Can you see the strawberry mark on his shoulder?

ELIZABETH. Clear as day. Oh, it's a beautiful strawberry mark.

BIRDIE. (*Tugging at* ELIZABETH's *skirt*) I want to see for myself.

ELIZABETH. He has such big muscles. Oh, do you know what he's doing now?

NETTIE. What?

LUCY. Tell us.

ELIZABETH. Calisthenics!

AMANTHA. What kind?

ELIZABETH. With big dumbbells. He's swinging them up . . . and down . . . and out . . . and back (*She gestures with her free arm*).

NETTIE. Oh, I can just picture him.

ELIZABETH. He's stopped for a minute now. He's inhaling. Oh, you should see his chest.

BIRDIE. (*Squealing with delight and tugging again*) I want to see it with my own eyes.

ELIZABETH. (*Fighting against the tugging*) He's squaring his shoulders. Oh, his shoulders . . . they're so broad.

AMANTHA. Don't torture us, Elizabeth.

ELIZABETH. Now he's flexing his biceps. (*Bending her free arm*) They're swelling up . . . and up . . . and up . . .

LUCY. (*Putting her fingers in her ears*) Oh, stop it! I can't stand it any more.

HILDEGARDE. (*Tugging at* ELIZABETH's *skirt*) Give me those binoculars.

AMANTHA. (*Tugging too*) We should all have a turn.

(*They all start tugging at* ELIZABETH's *skirt and reaching for the binoculars.*)

BIRDIE. They're my binoculars.

HILDEGARDE. It's my window, because it's my house.

AMANTHA. But it's my turn.

ELIZABETH. (*Resists, then suddenly lowers the binoculars*) Never mind now. He's finished with his exercises and he's disappeared. (*She climbs down from the chair as the rest scatter glumly*). It was a grand sight. If we could just afford more powerful binoculars . . .

BIRDIE. (*Ecstatically*) I'd like to *really* see him.

LUCY. We've sat on the porch, and watched him go in and out.

BIRDIE. But I mean *really* see him. Up close!

ELIZABETH. So would I. Why, we don't even know what color his eyes are.

LUCY. If you don't know, nobody knows. You have the binoculars most of the time.

BIRDIE. I'd like to hear his voice too.

NETTIE. Well, how can we get close to him unless we actually go across the street and . . . and . . .

HILDEGARDE. And what, Nettie?

NETTIE. Couldn't we pay him a neighborly visit?

HILDEGARDE. Nettie, *nice* ladies do *not* go visiting gentlemen.

ELIZABETH. Well, let's invite him to tea.

HILDEGARDE. That would be improper, inviting a gentleman to tea when we haven't been introduced.

NETTIE. Well, what can we do then?

AMANTHA. (*Suddenly and excited*) We'll have to make him come over here and visit us. We'll have to *arrange* it somehow.

NETTIE. How?

LUCY. If he was a plumber, we could stop up the sink.

ELIZABETH. If he was an electrician, we could blow a fuse.

AMANTHA. (*Grimly*) But he's not a plumber or an electrician. He's a detective in Homicide.

NETTIE. (*Looking around stupidly*) Well, how can we arrange for a detective in Homicide to come to this house?

AMANTHA. That's simple. All we need is a body.

NETTIE. A body?

AMANTHA. A dead body, that is.

ELIZABETH. Well, where on earth are we going to get a dead body?

(The ladies all look at ELIZABETH, *freezing into a tableau. Then the stage area blacks out, and all the light that remains is that from the desk lamp.* O'FINN *leans over the desk.)*

O'FINN. I wasn't there, Captain, but that's the way I've reconstructed how it happened. You can see, can't you? It was no fault of mine, except leaving the shade up.

WILLIAMS. Are you trying to tell me that it was just for the sake of your charming company that. . . ?

O'FINN. I'm not meaning to boast, Captain. I wouldn't have believed it myself. But the poor dears were so desperately lonesome. Spinsters every one, and getting a little old and touched in the head.

WILLIAMS. *(Digging through the pile of papers again)* I think I still have your report on this case. *(Gives up)* Well, I can't seem to find it now. You'll have to refresh my memory. What happened?

O'FINN. It wasn't long, sir, before there was a dead body sure enough. *(From the blacked-out stage area comes a crash of breaking dishes and a feminine scream.)* But by the time they called Homicide and Kramer and I got there . . . Well, the scene of the crime looked like . . . well, like nothing I ever saw before.

(The lights come up on the stage. ELIZABETH *lies dead on the sofa. She is arranged somewhat like a corpse in a coffin, except that her get-up is gay, not somber. The other ladies gather about admiringly.)*

AMANTHA. Doesn't she look pretty?

HILDEGARDE. I must admit it was very generous of all of you to give her your best things to wear.

NETTIE. She deserves it. Wasn't it nice of her, giving us this chance to meet Mr. O'Finn?

AMANTHA. Yes, that's why I sacrificed my precious pearls.

LUCY. Isn't my hat becoming to her?

NETTIE. Do you think they'll bury her in my feather boa?

BIRDIE. I suppose so. All those pretty things gone to waste. No . . . I didn't mean that. Forgive and forget. I'll just give her a little whiff of my perfume that she was always trying to steal. (*Sprays the corpse with an atomizer*)

(*The doorbell rings.*)

NETTIE. It must be him!

BIRDIE. I'm going to swoon!

HILDEGARDE. Don't you dare! Everybody behave themselves. Line up for introductions. And nobody step on those dishes I dropped. Remember the rule. Nothing must be touched at the scene of the crime. (*They line up in a sort of reception line with* ELIZABETH *as the last one in line.*)

NETTIE. We touched the body.

AMANTHA. We had to. Elizabeth went and got herself poisoned in her worst old house dress.

(*Doorbell rings again.*)

BIRDIE. Isn't somebody going to the door?

HILDEGARDE. I will.

(*She crosses Up Left to the front door and admits* KRAMER, *a small, sardonic plainclothes detective.*)

HILDEGARDE. I thought Mr. O'Finn was coming.

KRAMER. My name's Kramer. O'Finn's parking the car.

O'FINN. (*To* WILLIAMS) And that, Captain, was when I walked into the trap. (*He crosses Up Left to the front door, pantomiming an entrance and getting into the spirit of the play-within-a-play.*) Well, what have we here?

HILDEGARDE. (*Walking past* KRAMER *and ignoring him*) Mr. O'Finn?

O'FINN. That's myself. Now is this the house where the lady died?

HILDEGARDE. It is.

O'FINN. (*Doesn't see the sofa*) Where's the body?

HILDEGARDE. (*Aside to the ladies, but loud enough for O'FINN to hear*) Isn't he masterful? (*Grabbing his hand*) I'm Hildegarde Hodge, Mr. O'Finn. This is my house. I'm the one who called.

O'FINN. How do you do?

HILDEGARDE. (*Holding onto his hand and peering up into his face*) Oh, you poor boy. You look a little peakéd. Haven't been eating the right things, have you? That's the way with you bachelors.

O'FINN. Bachelor?

HILDEGARDE. (*Alarmed*) You're not married, are you?

O'FINN. Well, no . . .

HILDEGARDE. Good. Then you're unattached.

O'FINN. Now look, lady, you're not supposed to be asking questions, I am. Where's the body?

HILDEGARDE. First you must meet my boarders. This is Nettie Norton. (O'FINN *is propelled down the receiving line, and each lady grasps his hand as he goes by and scrutinizes him closely.*)

NETTIE. Oh, you have such a strong grip, Mr. O'Finn.

O'FINN. I'm sorry. Did I hurt you?

NETTIE. Oh no! I loved it! I felt just like I was one of your dumbbells.

HILDEGARDE. (*Sharply*) Nettie!

O'FINN. What's this?

AMANTHA. (*Grabbing his hand away*) I'm Amantha Abernathy. Oh, you are strong, Mr. O'Finn. Squeeze a little harder.

O'FINN. What?

AMANTHA. I wouldn't mind a little bruise.

O'FINN. (*Withdrawing his hand in alarm*) Honest, lady, I didn't mean to . . .

AMANTHA. That's the way with you he-men. You don't know your own strength.

LUCY. (*Grabbing his hand*) I'm Lucy Long. Mr. O'Finn, you remind me of my Herbert.

O'FINN. Who?

LUCY. A beau of mine. But he's dead now.

O'FINN. I'm sorry to hear that.

LUCY. Oh, that's all right. I'm out of mourning now.

Besides, he wasn't nearly as handsome as you are. (*Losing self-control*) Oh, Mr. O'Finn, you are handsome!

BIRDIE. Lucy, you're a bold hussy. (*Grabbing his hand*) Mr. O'Finn, I'm Birdie Beauregard. (*She begins to totter.*)

O'FINN. What's the matter?

BIRDIE. I feel like swooning.

O'FINN. Will somebody get her a glass of water or something?

BIRDIE. Would you catch me if I swooned?

O'FINN. Well, yeah, I guess so . . .

BIRDIE. In your strong, muscular arms?

HILDEGARDE. Birdie, show him Elizabeth.

BIRDIE. (*Gesturing*) Mr. O'Finn, this is Elizabeth Ellsworth.

(O'FINN *sees the corpse for the first time.* KRAMER *joins him beside the sofa.* O'FINN *takes the corpse's pulse.*)

KRAMER. Is she dead?

NETTIE. We wouldn't have given her all our pretty things if she was alive, would we?

O'FINN. (*Straightening*) She's dead all right. Kramer, call the meat wagon. Probably heart attack or something. (*To the ladies*) Ladies, I'm afraid you made a mistake in calling Homicide. You see, every time somebody keels over dead, we're not supposed to come and look at the body. It's only if the death has occurred under suspicious circumstances. Natural death isn't in our line. Let's go, Kramer.

LUCY. (*Quickly*) That wasn't a natural death!

NETTIE. She was poisoned!

AMANTHA. Murdered!

O'FINN. What? Who says she was murdered?

AMANTHA. We all do. (*They all nod solemnly.*)

O'FINN. What makes you think so?

LUCY. Elizabeth was as healthy and as strong as a horse. She didn't just keel over. You have the doctor do a . . . what's that they do?

AMANTHA. An autopsy.

LUCY. That's right. Autopsy. And then you'll see.

O'FINN. What makes you so sure? Who did it? (*There is a gale of giggles from the ladies.*) Did you all do it together?

BIRDIE. I didn't.

NETTIE. I didn't either.

AMANTHA. Mr. O'Finn, you're supposed to find out who did it. You're a detective.

O'FINN. Now wait a minute. You're sure there was a murder? Well, then, let's pretend there was one. You all didn't do it together, but you all know which one of you did?

LUCY. Oh no, we don't know.

NETTIE. It's a mystery.

HILDEGARDE. The one who did it knows, of course.

AMANTHA. Oh, yes, of course. She knows. But nobody else.

O'FINN. (*Aside to* KRAMER) Are they playing a game, or what?

KRAMER. (*Shrugs*) One thing for sure, that's a real body.

O'FINN. Maybe then we'd better get the facts just in case.

KRAMER. You're the boss.

O'FINN. (*Back to the ladies*) All right now, I'm going to ask a few questions.

BIRDIE. (*Squealing with joy*) We're going to get the third degree.

O'FINN. We'll start with the body. You didn't find it here, decked out like this.

LUCY. We had to dress Elizabeth up for the occasion.

KRAMER. Occasion? What occasion?

LUCY. Gentleman callers.

KRAMER. (*At* O'FINN) Oh yeah, sure.

AMANTHA. We couldn't leave her sprawled on the floor in her old house dress with gentlemen coming.

O'FINN. If there's been a murder, nothing should be touched at the scene of the crime.

BIRDIE. (*Aside to the ladies*) Isn't he wonderful when he's mad?

NETTIE. (*To the ladies*) I told you so. We didn't do it right.

AMANTHA. We didn't touch everything. (*Pointing*) There are the broken dishes Hildegarde dropped when she discovered the body.

O'FINN. (*To* HILDEGARDE) You discovered the body?

HILDEGARDE. I was bringing in the tea things, and I found Elizabeth on the floor.

O'FINN. And you were so surprised you dropped the dishes?

LUCY. And then she screamed. We heard her upstairs.

NETTIE. And we kind of knew what it meant. (*The other ladies give her warning looks.*)

O'FINN. What is all this? (*But the only answer he receives is another gale of giggles. He looks around for something to vent his anger and impatience upon.*) Kramer, pick up those broken dishes and put 'em in a box and label 'em "Exhibit A."

KRAMER. Where will I get a box?

HILDEGARDE. In the kitchen. (*Points*) That way.

(KRAMER *exits to the kitchen.*)

O'FINN. (*Pacing authoritatively*) Well now, there was a murder, was there? And one of you in this room committed the murder.

NETTIE. Who else?

O'FINN. Now the thing to look for in any murder is the motive. (KRAMER *enters with a small box, gets down on his hands and knees, and starts to collect the broken china.*) Now who would want to murder this poor lady here?

NETTIE. Somebody had to be murdered. And I'm glad it was Elizabeth.

O'FINN. (*Pouncing*) So! And what did you have against Elizabeth?

NETTIE. Well, she was selfish with the binoculars.

O'FINN. Binoculars? What's this about binoculars?

HILDEGARDE. Shame on you, Nettie!

NETTIE. I'm sorry. (*Starts to cry*)

O'FINN. Come on now. Out with it. What's the business about binoculars?

KRAMER. (*Looking up, sees binoculars on table, and*

points to them.) Hey, O'Finn, maybe that's what they're talking about.

O'FINN. (*Crosses to table and picks up the binoculars*) Well, here they are, but what do you mean?

BIRDIE. (*Giggling*) Don't make us tell you that, dear Mr. O'Finn.

O'FINN. Kramer, what do you think?

KRAMER. You use 'em to look through. (O'FINN *uses them, but looks at things inside the room.*) Hey, O'Finn, long-distance specs like that are for looking at things outdoors.

O'FINN. (*Uses the binoculars to look out the window*) The only thing I can see from here is my apartment building. I can even see my own windows.

HILDEGARDE. Girls, come and help me in the kitchen now. It's time for tea. (*They all run out to the kitchen, giggling louder than ever.*)

KRAMER. (*Tries to rise to his feet, doubled up with laughter*) O'Finn, O'Finn . . . I just made a brilliant deduction. I see the gimmick. Don't you?

O'FINN. What are you talking about?

KRAMER. You're supposed to be a detective, Dennis my lad. But it's your modesty that's blinding you. Now here are these poor old dames, with nothing to do all day but sit around. So one of 'em has a pair of these sailors' glasses, and they spend their time looking out the window with 'em, minding everybody else's business 'cause they don't have any business of their own. And what do they see straight across the street? A window. And what's in the window? A man. And what finer specimen of manhood is there than an Irish cop? Ah, you're a beautiful creature to behold, Dennis O'Finn. They're all in love with you.

O'FINN. Shut up!

KRAMER. (*Undaunted*) But how can these old biddies lure you across the street? You, a detective in Homicide. Elementary, my dear O'Finn.

O'FINN. It's a dirty lie!

KRAMER. You're the motive for this murder.

O'FINN. You can't prove that!

KRAMER. Do you want proof? Well, here it comes.

(*The ladies march in from the kitchen. They're carrying
a tea pot, cups, saucers, trays of biscuits, etc.*)

HILDEGARDE. We're having a party, Mr. O'Finn.

LUCY. Don't you worry, Mr. O'Finn, we opened a fresh
package of tea. I'm sure there's no rat poison in this.

HILDEGARDE. I'm using my best tea things, Mr. O'Finn.
But there are only six cups. There isn't any for Mr. Kramer.

KRAMER. I can take a hint. (*Starting to exit*) Six is
company, and seven's a crowd. I think I'll have a beer on
my way home. Ta ta, Dennis darlin'. Don't drink too much
tea. It's terrible strong stuff.

(O'FINN *throws the binoculars aside, and strides angrily down to the apron. The stage lights black out,
and* KRAMER's *laughter gradually subsides in the
darkness.*)

WILLIAMS. Kramer was right? They committed murder
just to get you inside their house?

O'FINN. (*Dejected*) It seems like it, Captain.

WILLIAMS. Did you conduct an investigation?

O'FINN. I did, Captain. There was arsenic rat poison in
the house. The dead woman had drunk it in her tea. She always sneaked down to the kitchen and stole an extra cup
of tea in the afternoon. So somebody had just mixed the
rat poison in the tea and it was waiting for her.

WILLIAMS. Who was guilty?

O'FINN. Well, that wasn't easy to find out. They didn't
try to help me much, because they wanted to keep me
hanging around. So I tried some strategy. I told 'em I de-
cided there hadn't been a murder after all, and I wasn't
coming back any more.

WILLIAMS. How did that strategy work?

O'FINN. Miserable, Captain, miserable.

(*The stage lights come on suddenly.* HILDEGARDE, BIRD-
IE, AMANTHA *and* LUCY *are sitting around the tea table, which has on it a tea pot, cups, saucers, etc. The
ladies look rather gloomy.*)

HILDEGARDE. It's been a whole week now.

AMANTHA. A whole week and not a glimpse of him. Going in and out of his apartment the back way, and keeping his shades down.

LUCY. We ought to complain to the police.

BIRDIE. We don't want to get Mr. O'Finn in trouble.

LUCY. But Elizabeth really was murdered, and Mr. O'Finn ought to be right here this minute investigating.

AMANTHA. We're just going to have to do what we talked about.

LUCY. You mean, we need another murder?

AMANTHA. Well, Mr. O'Finn couldn't pretend that two ladies poisoned in the same house was just a coincidence.

BIRDIE. Oh dear. Who shall it be? Nettie?

AMANTHA. She's the most convenient. She's always the last to come downstairs to tea.

BIRDIE. Poor Nettie. She's such a kind soul. She's the only one of you I really like.

AMANTHA. If you'd rather we'd use you, dear . . .

BIRDIE. Well, I wouldn't want to miss the fun when Mr. O'Finn comes back.

AMANTHA. It'll have to be Nettie then.

BIRDIE. All right, but after this, we'll have to get some new boarders. I'd rather we poison a stranger any time.

LUCY. Do we have any more poison? Mr. O'Finn took our old can of rat poison as "Exhibit B."

HILDEGARDE. I bought a new one.

AMANTHA. Fine. Go get it, Hildegarde. And I have a suggestion. Let's all hide our eyes. Then everybody walk over to the tea table one at a time. And whoever poisoned Elizabeth can put a spoonful of poison into Nettie's cup.

(HILDEGARDE *exits to the kitchen.*)

BIRDIE. (*Clapping*) Oh, goodie! Then it'll still be a mystery.

LUCY. Let's hurry before Nettie gets here.

(HILDEGARDE *enters from the kitchen with the rat poi son, places it on the tea table. The others range them ·*

selves around the wall, faces to the wall, away from
the table. HILDEGARDE *does likewise.*)

BIRDIE. Who's first?

HILDEGARDE. You, Birdie.

BIRDIE. (*Goes to the table, and stands downstage of it,*
facing upstage. All the ladies follow the same procedure.
Thus the audience can't see which of the ladies uses the
poison.) All right, I'm going. Now which one is Nettie's
cup?

HILDEGARDE. The one with the nick in the rim. She did
that herself, and I can't afford to always be buying new
cups.

AMANTHA. For pity's sake, Birdie, put the poison in the
right cup.

BIRDIE. (*Giggling on her way back*) What a perfect
chance for a double cross. How do you like that? Double
cross. That's slang among criminals. Of course I didn't
poison anybody. I couldn't even poison a rat.

LUCY. Oh, don't play innocent. Are you finished?

BIRDIE. Yes, I'm back home. (*Facing a wall*) It's your
turn, Lucy.

LUCY. (*Starting, then stopping*) I don't need to go. I
couldn't use the poison. You all know I couldn't hurt a fly.

AMANTHA. You're not fooling anyone, Lucy. I've
known all along that you were the one who poisoned Elizabeth.

LUCY. That's not so!

HILDEGARDE. Stop teasing her, Amantha. Let's get this
over with. Hurry up, Lucy.

LUCY. (*Going*) All right, if you insist.

AMANTHA. Listen to her old bones creak.

LUCY. That isn't my bones. It's the floor. I'd like to poison you, Amantha. That's who I'd like to poison.

BIRDIE. Well, not today, Lucy. Let's save Amantha for
some other time.

AMANTHA. I don't think I'll drink any more tea in this
house. I don't trust anybody.

BIRDIE. All's fair in love and war.

HILDEGARDE. Lucy, aren't you finished yet. You've
taken long enough to poison all of us.

LUCY. (*Back and facing a wall*) I'm back at home base now, and I didn't use the poison.

AMANTHA. I'm starting now.

HILDEGARDE. Hurry up with it.

AMANTHA. (*Going*) I feel just like Lucrezia Borgia. (*Humming at her work*)

BIRDIE. Do you think she's doing it?

LUCY. Of course she is. She's bloodthirsty. She's the guilty one.

HILDEGARDE. Remember, my dears, the "guilty one" is the one who brought dear Mr. O'Finn into our midst.

BIRDIE. That's right. Thank you very much, guilty one, whoever you are.

AMANTHA. (*Back, and facing a wall*) I'm finished. Your turn, Hildegarde.

HILDEGARDE. (*Going*) I'm on my way. I'm the last one, so I'll take the rat poison and hide it.

BIRDIE. Good idea, Hildegarde. We shouldn't leave rat poison right on the table. It might make Nettie suspicious.

HILDEGARDE. (*Hides the poison*) All right, I'm finished now. Let's all sit, and do try to act normal.

AMANTHA. Just in time. I hear Nettie coming down the front stairs.

(*They are all sitting there when* NETTIE *enters from Up Left. She sees them, stops and pouts.*)

NETTIE. You've started without me again. I hope you've left a body some tea.

(*The stage lights black out, leaving only the small desk lamp burning.* O'FINN *paces angrily on the apron.*)

WILLIAMS. So they committed another murder to lure you to the house, did they, O'Finn?

O'FINN. That they did, Captain. And don't think I didn't take it to heart, being the motive for murder like I was. Well, they put in a call for me, and Kramer and I went back to the house. And you might have known it, there they were again . . . in their reception line . . . waiting for me . . .

(*The stage lights come up.* NETTIE *is arranged on the sofa in the same way* ELIZABETH *was. The other ladies are in their reception line.* KRAMER *stands Up Left.* O'FINN *rushes into the scene.*)

KRAMER. It's about time you're getting here, Dennis my boy. You should know by now this is our regular Tuesday stop.

O'FINN. Another one, eh?

AMANTHA. That's right, Mr. O'Finn. There's a murderer loose in this house. We demand police protection.

KRAMER. (*To* O'FINN) Looks to me like the police need the protection. But do you see what happens, Dennis, when you neglect your duty and don't come by this house for tea every day? Something always seems to get into the tea when you're not here.

O'FINN. Oh, you needn't remind me, Kramer. Well, this time I'm not going to budge from this place till I find out who's guilty.

BIRDIE. (*Clapping*) Oh, wonderful, Mr. O'Finn is going to live here with us.

LUCY. Do you think it would be proper? We've always had just lady boarders.

HILDEGARDE. It's up to me to say what's proper in this house.

BIRDIE. Oh please, let him stay, Hildegarde. There are two rooms vacant now. He could have his choice.

HILDEGARDE. We could see to it that he eats the right things, couldn't we? But he'd have to pay just like anyone else. In fact, he'd have to pay double because he'd eat twice as much.

AMANTHA. Oh, Hildegarde, you're so mercenary.

HILDEGARDE. I'm a poor woman.

LUCY. Poor! You're an old miser.

BIRDIE. Well then, if Mr. O'Finn has to pay double, he should have both rooms, and one could be his gymnasium. He could do his exercises there and we could watch . . . and we could see his strawberry mark again.

AMANTHA. Birdie!

O'FINN. Ladies . . . ladies . . . stop! Let's get down to business. Kramer, will you check and make sure we have a dead body. (KRAMER *crosses to the sofa and examines the corpse.*)

LUCY. Oh, she's dead all right. We can guarantee that.

O'FINN. Well, thank you. All right now, ladies, I want your attention. There'll be no more tea parties. There's been another murder, and I want to know who did it!

LUCY. Oh, we can't tell you. We don't know. Because we all hid our eyes.

O'FINN. (*Crossing to the sofa*) Kramer what kind of malarkey are they handing me now?

KRAMER. Don't you see, O'Finn? They're playing games. Like "hide and seek." And you're "it," pal. It's simple, like they said. Have you no imagination, man? One of 'em committed the murder while the rest of 'em hid their eyes. Sure, isn't that the usual way murders are always committed?

O'FINN. They're too dangerous to run loose. I'm going to call the paddy wagon and lock 'em all up.

KRAMER. (*Enjoying himself*) You can't do that, Dennis. You got to have evidence.

O'FINN. (*Moaning*) What evidence do I have?

KRAMER. (*Looks around, spots the box of broken dishes that is still sitting on a side table, crosses and picks it up.*) We still got "Exhibit A" from the first murder. A bunch of broken cups and saucers.

AMANTHA. You see how cooperative we are, Mr. O'Finn. We saved those for you.

O'FINN. (*Savagely*) It's a good thing you did, or I'd have had you all in the clink for destroying evidence.

LUCY. Is it really evidence?

O'FINN. (*Desperate*) Of course it is.

BIRDIE. A clue?

O'FINN. That's right.

BIRDIE. What does it mean?

KRAMER. That's what I'd like to know, O'Finn. What does it mean?

O'FINN. Now don't try to confuse me, Kramer. (*Groping*) It's just that . . . well, she dropped 'em in surprise when she found that first body, you see . . .

KRAMER. So what?

O'FINN. (*Still searching*) Well now, that's a funny

thing. (*Taking the box of broken dishes*) Here is a whole set of dishes, cups and saucers—broken. But you weren't short of dishes at all, Miss Hildegarde. On the day of the first murder, when I stayed and drank tea with you ladies, you brought out another set.

HILDEGARDE. Oh yes, I brought my best dishes for you, Mr. O'Finn.

O'FINN. I see. Your best set. (*Looking around*) This is your best set on the table here now, I suppose.

HILDEGARDE. Oh no, they're my second best. But I'll use my best ones every day when you're boarding here with us, Mr. O'Finn.

AMANTHA. Because every day will be a special day, Mr. O'Finn.

O'FINN. (*Hastily*) Hold everything. Don't be getting me off the track. Now let's see, your very best dishes are still in the cupboard, and these here on the table are your second best. So these broken ones here in this box must have been your third best. Ah hah!

KRAMER. Are you onto something, O'Finn?

O'FINN. I may be, Kramer. I may be at that. Let's have a good look at these broken dishes. (*The two detectives start examining the contents of the box.*) Kramer, do you notice something funny about this junk?

KRAMER. How do you mean?

O'FINN. Ah, you'll never make a detective, Kramer. Look at this stuff. Do you notice anything missing?

KRAMER. You mean there are some missing pieces?

O'FINN. Some very important missing pieces, my boy. There are no handles for any of the cups. (*Turning with mock savagery on* BIRDIE) Miss Birdie, I have a question to put to you.

BIRDIE. (*Fluttering*) Yes, Mr. O'Finn?

O'FINN. Miss Birdie, tell me something about this house. On days that are not special occasions, days when you are not having visitors, do you often drink your tea in cups without handles?

BIRDIE. Oh no, Mr. O'Finn, that wouldn't be ladylike.

O'FINN. Why did it happen then, that on the day of the first murder, Miss Hildegarde brought in cups without handles?

BIRDIE. I don't know.

O'FINN. (*Striding and facing downstage, and pounding a fist into a palm*) Well, I'll tell all of you why. Miss Hildegarde brought in cups without handles because she knew she was going to find a dead body, and knew she was going to pretend to be surprised by dropping the tray of dishes. (*Turns dramatically*) Miss Hildegarde Hodge, I arrest you for . . .

> (*He is interrupted by a deafening chorus of giggles coming from all the ladies, including even* HILDE-GARDE. *They talk, swiftly, almost all at once.*)

LUCY. Was it really you, Hildegarde?

HILDEGARDE. It was really me.

BIRDIE. I would never have thought of that clue of the cup handles. Isn't Mr. O'Finn clever?

AMANTHA. Marvelous. Mr. O'Finn, are you going to take Hildegarde to jail?

HILDEGARDE. Will you take me in your car, Mr. O'Finn? Do we have to take Mr. Kramer along?

BIRDIE. Oh, Hildegarde, you're the lucky one. I wish now I were guilty. If I'd just had the nerve! I'd give anything to ride with Mr. O'Finn in his car.

> (*They all converge on* O'FINN. *He raises both hands protectively around his head, as if being attacked by a swarm of bees, and strides down onto the apron, as the stage lights black out and the giggles gradually subside.*)

O'FINN. Let me out of here! (*Recovering in front of* WILLIAMS' *desk.*) Well, that's how it was, Captain.

WILLIAMS. But you got your murderer. Why should you have to resign from Homicide?

O'FINN. I wouldn't be bragging, but it was a neat bit of deduction, if I do say so. But the thing of it is now, I've solved the murders, and I won't be going back to that house any more. Remember what they did the last time when I started to ignore them. And the other ladies were jealous of Hildegarde, don't you see? Now one of 'em will be committing murder too, just to get attention. As I said, it's a matter of life and death.

WILLIAMS. Yes, I see.

O'FINN. To be on the safe side, I've already told 'em you approved the transfer, Captain. Girls, I said, if there's any more murders here, you'll have only the attentions of Mr. Kramer. This is my last case in Homicide. As of to-day, I'm transferring over to the Arson Squad.

(There is the sound of a siren, and KRAMER *enters from the wings Down Left.)*

KRAMER. Hey, O'Finn, you in Arson yet?

O'FINN. I don't know. What about it, Captain? Am I in Arson?

WILLIAMS. *(Signing the paper)* You're in Arson, O'Finn. Transfer is approved.

KRAMER. Well, I wanted to be sure. 'Cause I just heard it on the short-wave. Big fire. Old house. Right across the street from your apartment, O'Finn.

(Complete black out.)

Also By
C.B Gilford

Bull In a China Shop

Jury Room

Who Dunit?

OTHER TITLES AVAILABLE FROM BAKER'S PLAYS

JURY ROOM

C.B. Gilford

Drama / 5m, 7f / Interior

Twelve jurors gather to decide the innocence or guilt of a young girl. Did she stab her uncle in cold blood? Eleven jurors say Yes — one, a student actress, says No. The jurors agree to her request to re-enact the crime right there. Props are brought in — including the actual murder weapon. The actress becomes the accused. The foreman takes the part of the murdered man, and as the re-enactment proceeds, some people begin to lose themselves in their parts. It's a tense situation, for if the girl did not kill her uncle — who did? Could it even be one of the characters on stage? The verdict, the solution, and the climax of the play arrive together in a single, smashing conclusion!

OTHER TITLES AVAILABLE FROM BAKER'S PLAYS

WHO DUNIT?

C.B. Gilford

Genre / Characters/ Set

Who Dunit? first ran as a short story in *Ellery Queen's Mystery Magazine*, and was later a hit on "Alfred Hitchcock Presents", translated into a dozen foreign languages, reprinted in several anthologies. What happens when a famous mystery writer is murdered, goes to Heaven and discover's that not even St. Michael knows who murdered him? There's only one answer: Saint Michael sends him back to earth to relive the past twenty-four hours of his life in order to solve the murder before it is committed. The writer discovers everybody he knows has a good reason to kill him! And then—is he just going to sit there and let it happen a second time? So the writer must outwit both the murderer and the Archangel Michael.

MYSTERY, MAYHEM, AND MURDER!

Jed Parish

4m, 7f / Interior

Domineering Juliet Brighton decides to have the town house done over and orders meek husband Boniface to have their summer house opened. But mysterious things begin to happen when they settle down in their country home. Loud, mocking laughter is heard, and a woman's body is discovered in the living room. Suddenly, the lights go out, and when they flash on again the body has disappeared!

OTHER TITLES AVAILABLE FROM BAKER'S PLAYS

ALICE IN AMERICA-LAND
or *Through the Picture Tube and What Alice Found There*

Dennis Snee

Comedy Fantasy / Flexible / Open Stage with Backdrops

In this fresh and lively update of Lewis Carroll's classic, Alice takes a journey through the picture tube of her family's television, and meets a mad collection of characters — with a certain difference! A White Rabbit — who lives in fear of someone's dropping "the big one." A Mock Turtle — who's a champion of consumer rights. A Dodo who's a guitarist, a Dormouse seeking political office and an Eagle who lives in the past. The Duke and Duchess have switched life roles — she's a "working duchess" while he's a "house duke." Alice herself becomes the unwitting subject for a showbiz roast with two aging, bitter comedians — the Mad Hatter and the March Hare. Through it all, Alice just wants to return home to her beloved cat. Just when it seems as though this mad world of America-land will drive her as mad as the inhabitants, she awakens, safe at home, her cat in her lap. A fanciful, biting, always funny tale of a contemporary Alice that will delight all audiences.

Lightning Source UK Ltd.
Milton Keynes UK
UKOW06f0343200116

266734UK00001B/20/P